the first snowfall

BY ANNE ROCKWELL   ILLUSTRATED BY HARLOW ROCKWELL

ALADDIN · New York · London · Toronto · Sydney · New Delhi

❧ ALADDIN

An imprint of Simon & Schuster Children's Publishing Division

1230 Avenue of the Americas, New York, NY 10020

This Aladdin hardcover edition November 2014

Copyright © 1987 by Anne Rockwell and Harlow Rockwell

Jacket illustration © 2014 by Lizzy Rockwell

For information about special discounts for bulk purchases, please contact Simon & Schuster Special Sales at 1-866-506-1949 or business@simonandschuster.com.

The Simon & Schuster Speakers Bureau can bring authors to your live event. For more information or to book an event contact the Simon & Schuster Speakers Bureau at 1-866-248-3049 or visit our website at www.simonspeakers.com.

Designed by Jessica Handelman

The text of this book was set in Kindergarten.

The illustrations for this book were rendered in pencil and watercolor.

Manufactured in China 0814 SCP

10 9 8 7 6 5 4 3 2 1

Library of Congress Cataloging-in-Publication Data

Rockwell, Anne F.

The first snowfall.

Summary: A child enjoys the special sights and activities of a snow-covered world.

1. Snow—Juvenile literature.

[1. Snow] I. Rockwell, Harlow. II. Title.

QC929.S7R63   1987   86-23712

ISBN 978-1-4814-1135-6

ISBN 978-1-4814-1402-9 (eBook)

With appreciation and thanks to the Children's Literature Research Collections, University of Minnesota Libraries, Minneapolis, for use of Harlow Rockwell's original *The First Snowfall* artwork.

I saw the snow begin to fall.

Snow fell and fell
all through the cold and quiet night.

In the morning, I put on red mittens,
a plaid muffler, my wooly cap, and warm boots

with my new ski jacket
and pants.

Then I went outside in the snow.

I waved to the driver
of the snowplow
when it came down our street.

This is the snow shovel I used

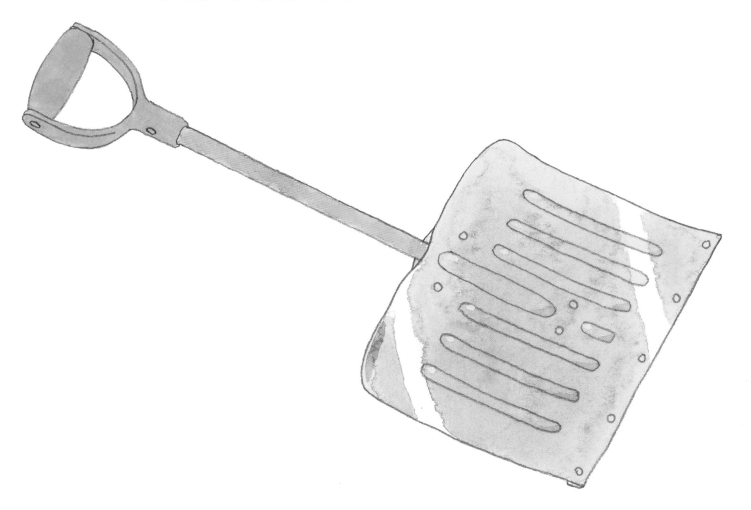

to shovel a path through the snow.

This is the snowball I rolled

to build our snowman.

Our car was covered with snow
until we brushed it off.

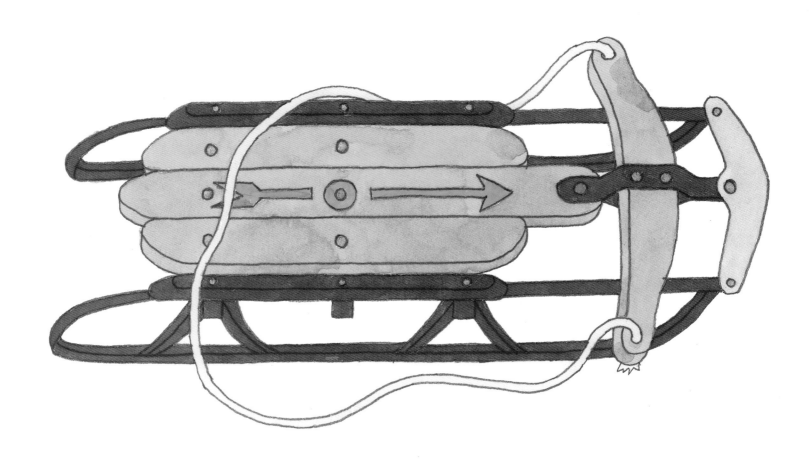

This is the sled we put in the car.

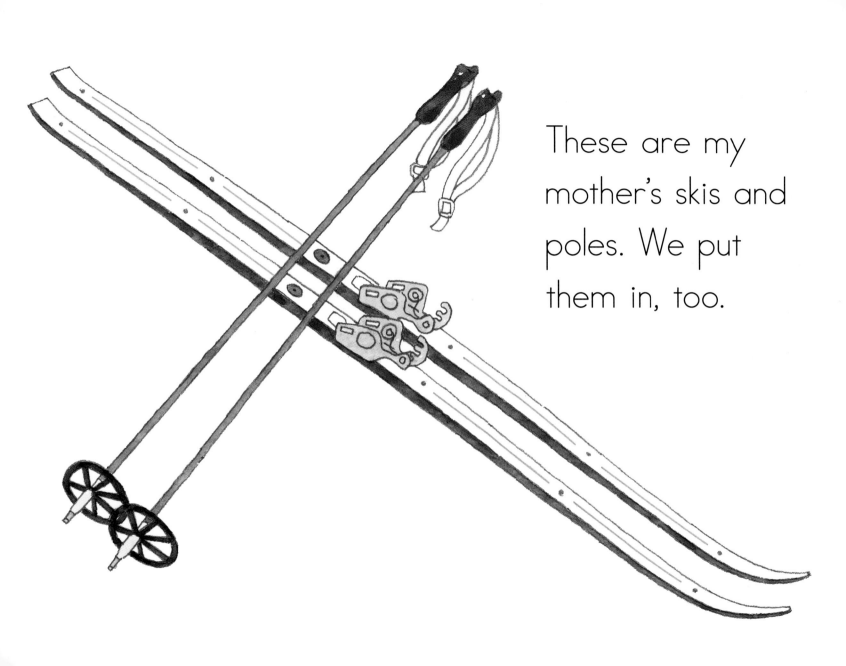

These are my
mother's skis and
poles. We put
them in, too.

At the park,
I rode
on the sled
with my father.

My mother skied across the hills
all covered with snow.

This is the hot cocoa I drank when I came home.

It warmed me up.

Then I went outside to play in the snow some more.